| DATE DUE | | | |
|---|---|---|---|
| | | | |
| | | | |
| | | | |
| | | | |
| | | | |
| | | | |
| | | | |
| | | | |
| | | | |
| | | | |
| | | | |
| | | | |
| | | | |
| | | | |

# HEATHER, BELLE OF THE BALL
## by Sheri Cooper Sinykin

Cover by
### Richard Lauter

Illustrations by
### Ed Tadiello

Spot Illustrations by
### Rich Grote

MAGIC ATTIC PRESS

As members of the
MAGIC ATTIC CLUB,
we promise to
be best friends,
share all of our adventures in the attic,
use our imaginations,
have lots of fun together,
and remember—the real magic is in us.

Alison    Keisha

Heather    Megan

# Table of Contents

# PARTY PLANS

Heather! Look out!"

Just as Heather Hardin turned toward her friend Alison, who stood on the other side of the tetherball pole, the careening ball smacked her squarely in the face. Leaving their places in line, Megan and Keisha rushed to Heather's side.

Alison did, too. "Heather, I'm sorry. Are you okay? Let me see," said Alison, peeling Heather's hand away.

"Well, your nose isn't bleeding," Keisha reported, "but

you might have a shiner by tomorrow."

The skin around Heather's left eye felt warm and tingly. Keisha was probably right about that shiner.

"I tried to warn you." Alison gave an apologetic shrug. "What were you looking at, anyway?"

"Nothing."

Megan laughed. "Don't you mean nobody?" She crooked her thumb in the direction of Tiffany Sibbett and her little knot of friends. "Forget her, Heather. You know we're not going to be invited to her big-deal birthday party."

"We don't know that," Heather said. "Tiffany's nice. Why wouldn't she invite us?"

"Oh, Heather." Megan sighed. She, Keisha, and Alison exchanged a glance that made Heather wish she'd lived here forever. Then she'd know everything about everyone, the way her best friends seemed to.

"But it would be fun to go to Majesty on Ice, wouldn't it?" Heather persisted. "Maybe we'd even get our pictures in the paper, like Tiffany and her friends did last year."

"So they rode a circus elephant," said Alison. "The paper couldn't even spell their names right."

"Yeah," Keisha chimed in, "and if Tiffany wasn't

always waving that sorry old clipping in everybody's face, you'd never have even known about it, Heather."

But to Heather, Tiffany and her friends seemed cool. She couldn't understand what Megan and the others had against them.

Keisha touched Heather's arm, pulling her from her thoughts. "Maybe we should take you to the nurse," she suggested. "She'll have an ice pack."

"Good idea," said Alison. When Heather started to protest, she flashed her infectious grin and added, "No arguments." For a moment, she sounded just like Heather's mother.

"Can't hurt, I guess." Flanked by her friends, Heather started across the playground. Daffodils and tulips blazed beneath the classroom windows. She should have been paying attention to her tetherball game. *Especially* with Alison, who was such a strong competitor. Now she was making them all miss recess—and it was one of the first perfect-weather days of the year.

With a sigh, Heather glanced over her shoulder at Tiffany. To her surprise, the shaggy-haired blond was jogging toward her. "Heather, wait!" Tiffany called. "Why are you going in?"

Heather and her own friends stopped. "What's it to her?" Alison muttered.

"Don't anyone tell her the truth," Heather whispered. "Please? I'm so embarrassed."

Keisha patted Heather on the back. "Leave it to me." She grinned as Tiffany drew closer. "Hey, Tiff! What's up?"

"I can't believe you're all going in already. It's so nice out here."

"Yeah, well, we can only handle so much *nice*, you know?" Keisha cast Heather a hint of a smile. Megan bit back a giggle.

Tiffany frowned as if she didn't quite understand.

"Well, anyway . . ." She shook her head, and her hair fell in perfect layers. "Oh, Heather. I've got a copy of that article about your mom. Remind me when we get back to the room. It's in my desk."

"Thanks." Heather raised an eyebrow at Alison that said, See? She's not so bad.

Tiffany simply smiled, nudged her friends, and headed back toward the playground.

"Her and her newspaper clippings!" said Keisha. "Come on. Let's get you some ice."

"Hey, I've got an idea," Alison said. "Let's have our *own* special party the same night as Tiffany's. A sleep over, with double-pepperoni pizza and games and movies."

Keisha nodded enthusiastically. "Who needs Tiffany Sibbett, anyway?"

"Not us!" chimed in Megan. "We're the Magic Attic Club. We make our own fun."

"*That's* the truth." Heather grinned, remembering how the four of them had first visited Ellie Goodwin's attic, gone on an amazing adventure through her mirror, and formed the Magic Attic Club. Ellie had invited them to return and go on other adventures any time they wanted. Maybe they'd even go again the night of the party . . .

"We could probably have it at my house," Alison offered. "I just have to check first with my mom."

11

"No offense, Ali," said Keisha, "but can you keep your brothers out of our pizza?"

"Hmmm. I see your point." Alison pulled the door open and the others went inside the school. "I know. Maybe we could have it at Megan's."

"Perfectamundo!" Megan's green eyes lit up at the suggestion. "No brothers. No sisters. And Aunt Frances wouldn't even *think* of eating our pizza."

"Heather?" Keisha stopped walking. "What's the matter? You haven't said a word."

"Nothing's the matter," Heather insisted. "The party's a great idea. Really. It'll be fun."

Keisha cocked her head and frowned. "You sure?"

"What could be better than being with my very best friends?" But Heather's smile felt lopsided. Her eye was watering. Gingerly, she touched the area around it. She'd be fine once she had that ice pack.

# Two

# MAIL FOR HEATHER

Heather flipped through the stack of advertisements and envelopes on the kitchen counter. She wondered why she even bothered to look. Old friends were more likely to phone than to write. There was never any mail for her. She was about to nudge the pile aside when, stuck inside a sale notice, a pretty envelope caught her eye.

She squinted at the fancy handwriting, then checked for a return address. There was nothing on the front, but she could feel raised letters on the back flap. Turning the envelope over, she read:

SIBBETT
741 LAKESHORE LANE

"Omigosh!" Heather gasped. Opening the envelope neatly with a knife, she pulled out a glossy white card trimmed with tiny bows. "Mom! Jenna! I'm invited. Come look!"

When no one came running, Heather grabbed the hand-lettered invitation and raced upstairs. She found them in her older sister's room, where Jenna was interviewing Mom for a report she was writing.

"Look!" Heather waved the card at them. "It's from Tiffany! For her birthday party. The ice show, remember? I didn't think she liked me, but . . ." Her voice trailed off.

What if Keisha, Megan, and Alison weren't invited? And what about the party they all were planning?

"What's not to like, Heather?" Mom smiled.

"Jen, isn't that cool?"

"Tiffany who? Sibbett?"

At Heather's nod, Jenna

14

continued, "I know her brother. He's okay, I guess. It's too bad he can't buy himself a personality, though."

Casting Jenna a disapproving glance, her mother turned to Heather. "When's the party, Heather?" she asked.

"A week from tomorrow."

Heather's mother looked thoughtful. "Hmm. Same night as that Children's Hospital charity auction I was asked to donate to. Which reminds me. I have to let them know my decision."

"Tell them no," Jenna said. "If you give away all your best stuff, how are you ever going to afford to send me away to college?" She flicked her wispy bangs off her forehead and smiled sweetly.

Heather supposed Jenna was kidding, because their parents never seemed all that worried about money. Still, college cost a lot—especially the fancy one Jenna hoped to get into. Maybe Mom *should* hold on to her paintings, just in case.

"Never you mind about college," Mrs. Hardin said. "Just worry about your grades and leave the rest to us."

Heather cleared her throat to get her mother's attention. "So? Can I go? Please, please?"

"Are the girls invited, too?"

Heather knew exactly which girls her mother meant. "I—I don't know. I have to call them." She fingered the bows on the invitation absently. "So, does that mean yes? You'll let me go?"

"I suppose so. And if Dad and I are at the auction and can't drive you, maybe one of the other girls' parents can."

Heather hugged her mother. Maybe she wouldn't need a ride. Or maybe the others would be invited, too.

The phone rang shrilly and, as Heather reached for it, Jenna gave her a pained look. "Heather, we're trying to work here," she said.

"You can take it in my room, hon." Heather sprinted down the hall to her parents' bedroom to beat the answering machine.

"Hi, Heather." It was Alison. "You want to come over and taste test my mom's new fruit tart recipe? Keisha and Megan are here, and we thought we'd make plans for our party."

Heather eyed the invitation guiltily. She simply ought to ask Alison whether she'd received one, too. But she was sure she knew the answer already. Asking would only hurt Alison's feelings. Still, what was wrong with having more than one group of friends?

"Heather?"

"Uh, I was just thinking about what homework I have."

"Aw, come on," said Alison. "You can do that later. This won't take long."

"Okay. I'll be right over." After tucking the invitation away in the top drawer of her nightstand, Heather told her mother where she was going and hurried across the street. Before she could even knock, Alison's little brothers came charging out the front door, their fists full of cookies. "Hi, guys," she said as they flew past.

A moment later, Alison appeared, her hands on her hips and her lips pressed into a tight line. She looked angry enough to breathe fire. How could Alison already know that Heather was going to Tiffany's party? "What's the matter, Ali?" she asked at last.

"Stevie and Jason just made off with all the cookies I baked yesterday! Every last one!" She stamped her foot.

Heather smiled, relieved. "Well," she said, "you can always make more. Take it as a compliment."

Alison's expression softened. She shook her head, broke into the famous McCann smile, and patted Heather on the back. "Thanks. You're right, and that's exactly what I'll do. Besides, what choice do I have?" She led Heather through the house and out to the porch.

Keisha and Megan, flanked by planters of bright flowers, were on the double swing. The pages of Megan's notebook riffled in the breeze as she chewed on her pen.

"Hey, Heather," called Keisha, "want us to scoot over?"

"No, that's okay." Heather flopped down onto one of the McCanns' comfy chaise longues. "What're the plans so far?" she asked.

"Nothing," replied Megan. "We were waiting for you."

Avoiding their eyes, Heather rubbed at a spot on her white tennis shoes. "Would you guys mind if we changed the party to *Saturday* night?"

"Why Saturday?" asked Alison. "I thought we agreed to have it the same night as Tiffany's."

"We did, only . . ." Heather's voice trailed off. She retied her shoe. "I'm not sure I can make it on Friday, that's all."

Keisha and Megan stopped swinging and exchanged a sideways glance. "Why?" Keisha asked. "What's up?"

# Chapter
## Three

# SOMETHING PINK

Heather debated whether just to come right out and tell them about Tiffany's party. They'd understand, wouldn't they? Then she thought of their conversation earlier at school. Maybe they wouldn't understand.

All of them were looking at her, waiting for her to say something. "Why can't we just have our party on Saturday? What's the big deal?"

Keisha folded her arms across her chest. She cocked her head, studying Heather. Then, ever so gently, she started the swing moving again. "Are you sure there's nowhere *else* you want to go on Friday?" she asked at last.

"Like maybe . . . Tiffany Sibbett's party?" Alison raised one eyebrow.

Heather sighed. "Okay, okay. So she *did* invite me."

"I knew it," Megan muttered.

"I didn't want to tell you," Heather went on, "because I didn't want to hurt your feelings. I was afraid you wouldn't be invited."

"We weren't," Keisha replied. "Not that we really care. What I don't get is, why do *you* care so much, Heather?"

Heather stalled. How could she explain it? "I—I don't know," she said, finally. "I guess I just want everybody to like me. What's wrong with that?"

"If that's true, then why are you leaving us?" asked Megan.

"Yeah, and—no offense—but what makes you think it's *you* Tiffany really likes?" Alison avoided Heather's eyes.

"What's that supposed to mean?" Heather snapped, drawing her legs up to her chest. She wished she could curl herself into a tiny ball and roll away.

"*You* tell, Keisha," Megan said softly. "You're the one who heard it."

"Heard what?"

Keisha began hesitantly. "Tiffany and those guys were

22

talking in the bathroom—about your mom and that article in the 'Lifestyle' section. And I guess they saw her TV interview, too. Anyway," she took a deep breath, "don't you see, Heather? They think you're cool, but it's not because of *you*, it's because of your mom. Tomorrow they'll decide someone else is cool and drop you like a rock."

Words wouldn't come. Heather struggled out of the chaise longue. All she wanted to do was run. Beyond the McCann's redwood fence, Ellie Goodwin's white Victorian house stood like a beacon.

"I'm sorry," Keisha said quickly. "I . . . we didn't want to hurt *your* feelings either."

"You're just jealous," Heather blurted, surprised at her own words.

"He*ather*!" Alison reached for her, but Heather pulled away.

"Us? Jealous? You've got to be kidding."

"Oh, get off it." She couldn't help the hard edge in her voice. "You guys wanted to go as much as I did and you know it."

"Heather, you don't really believe that, do you?" Megan asked.

"I don't know *what* to believe," replied Heather, and before she could think twice, she was stomping across the yard and out the side gate. If the others called after her, she didn't hear. As she ran toward the sidewalk, she tried to ignore the tightening knot in her stomach.

Instead of heading home, she veered toward Ellie's house. It's time to go to the attic, she thought. An adventure was exactly what she needed. Within moments, she was knocking on the older woman's door.

"Why, Heather, come in!" Ellie cried, stepping aside to let her pass. "It's good to see you."

At the sight of Ellie, resplendent in a sunflower-print dress, Heather forced a smile. "Hi, Ellie. Are you busy right now?"

"I was just going to take a break from my letter writing and fix some iced tea. Would you care to join me?"

Standing in the foyer now, Heather gazed longingly at the silver box on the table. "Well, I—"

Gently, Ellie raised Heather's chin so that her flame-blue eyes met Heather's. "Would you rather go on up to the attic, dear?"

Heather nodded. "You don't mind?"

"Not at all." Ellie smiled, then handed Heather the key from the silver box. "*Bon voyage!*"

"Thanks, Ellie. I knew you'd understand." Heather hurried up the stairs to the attic, her heart beating fast. After unlocking the door, her feet pounded up the next flight even faster. She could hardly wait to look through the trunk for an outfit to try on. What would happen this time?

Heather turned the fancy hanging lamp on. Before her, on the oriental rug, the great steamer trunk waited. She rushed forward to lift the lid.

A jumble of outfits greeted her. As she searched through the clothes, she wished she knew what she was looking for. Something pink, she thought. That would cheer her up. Within moments, her fingers closed around a crush of brilliant-hued organza.

Tugging on the material, Heather pulled forth a long, bright-pink ball gown with an elegant off-the-shoulder poof of fabric. A glittery gold belt adorned the waist. "This is perfect," she whispered. Remembering the tiara and the sequin-trimmed evening bag that Keisha had found on their first visit to the attic, Heather collected them from the mahogany wardrobe.

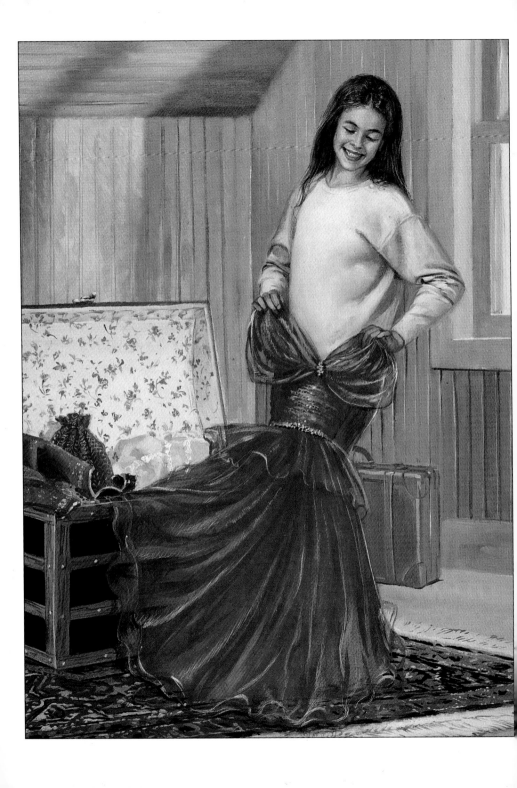

Before long she had pulled off her jeans and shirt and slipped into the ball gown. It swished about her as she waltzed toward the gilded mirror. Her breath caught as she glimpsed her reflection.

Her image in the shimmery dress seemed to shiver as if a draft had swept through the attic. Maybe one of the windows was open. Heather glanced about. When she again caught her reflection, she was not alone.

Chapter

*Four*

# A COUSIN'S GIFT

The attic had disappeared. A blond girl about Heather's age knelt beside her, inspecting the hem of the splendid ball gown. "Isn't it lovely, Miss? Are you surprised?" the girl asked in a lilting English accent. "Miss Catherine selected it personal. I am so glad it fits. It is rather late for alterations, isn't it?"

"Yes, I suppose it is," Heather said, playing along. Who in the world was Catherine?

She glanced about the warm, welcoming parlor in

which she now found herself. In each heavily draped window stood a mannequin in a fancy, old-fashioned gown that swept the carpet. Fine, floral-print paper covered the walls. Maybe she was in a dress shop, somewhere in England—though she had no idea what period of history she'd stumbled into. Women in long dark dresses bustled about with bolts of cloth, and measuring tapes, and pins. A freestanding three-way mirror stood to Heather's right. "I'm sorry," Heather said, "did you tell me your name?"

"Lisbeth." The girl tucked a strand of hair into the knot atop her head. "Lisbeth Atkins, Miss. At your service."

Heather noted the older clerks and patrons in the dress shop and laughed. "You're too young to be at my service. And please, call me Heather."

"Oh, but it's my job, Miss Heather." Lisbeth's cheeks flushed. "I am apprenticed to Mrs. Walters." She indicated the robust woman at the sales counter. "She has been so kind—almost like me mum, really—taking me out of the orphanage, letting me work in her shop. I shouldn't like to return to St. Philomena's, you know, and that's just where she'd send me if I forgot my place."

"St. Philomena's?" asked Heather.

"The orphanage!" Lisbeth suppressed a giggle. "Have you forgotten the ball, Miss Heather? Goodness,

after all the trouble your aunt and uncle went to, bringing you here?"

"I—It must be the journey," Heather hedged, not yet sure why she was here—wherever *here* was. "My mind has gone to mush."

"Surely you remember the charity ball for St. Philomena's!"

"Oh, yes. It's at . . ." Heather let her voice trail off, hoping Lisbeth would fill in the rest.

"Your aunt and uncle's country estate, of course. Have you never been there?"

Heather shook her head.

"You are so fortunate to have a cousin like Miss Catherine. She wanted to make certain you'd be the belle of the ball." Lisbeth gestured gracefully at Heather's gown. "She comes in here regular. Excellent taste she has, don't you think?"

Heather spun about, delighting in the swirl of organza. As she did, she noticed a gauzy garment hanging behind the dressing screen. It was pale and drab compared to the one Catherine had chosen for her. "This dress is certainly more appropriate than that one," commented Heather.

"More royal perhaps. But that dress also looked lovely on you. Any girl would be proud to wear it. Come. Let me wrap it for you. You'll take it along in the carriage."

"The carriage!" Heather tried to catch a glimpse of it through the window. Her own reflection distracted her. "I feel like a princess. Or maybe Cinderella."

Lisbeth smiled. "You Americans are not accustomed to such royal affairs. But the London Season is just starting, you know. Our shop will be very busy for months now."

"Don't you get a vacation?"

Lisbeth looked puzzled. "Oh, a holiday, you mean." She laughed lightly. "I should be glad for a change of scene. Maybe someday . . ."

Heather didn't miss her chance to ask Lisbeth about the social season and the royal affair to which she was apparently headed. She gathered that her relatives' estate was only a short ride away. As she and Lisbeth chatted, she couldn't help but feel sorry for the young shop girl. Surely she was more like Cinderella than Heather was. When Lisbeth reached for Heather's old dress to wrap it, Heather noticed the longing in the girl's pale-blue eyes.

"Please," Heather said, "why don't *you* keep it?"

"Oh, but I couldn't. Besides, where would I wear it?"

Heather's mind whirred. She could come up with only one answer. The more she thought about it, the more right it seemed—for her and for Lisbeth. "Why don't you come with me?"

"To the ball?"

"Why not? You'd be my guest. And it's not as if you don't already know Catherine, right?"

"Oh, but . . . could I really? Me? Lisbeth Atkins at the Spencer-Moultons'?"

Heather nodded eagerly. Wherever she was headed, she would be more at ease going with someone she knew, however slightly, someone who might be able to help her with the local customs. "Go ask Mrs. Walters."

Lisbeth spoke to the older woman, then disappeared for a moment. She returned with a hooded velvet cape that matched Heather's gown. "I almost forgot this," said Lisbeth. "Now you wait right here. I shall be ready in two shakes of a lamb's tail." When Lisbeth returned wearing the gauzy dress, Mrs. Walters was just locking up for the night. Heather gave Lisbeth the tiny bag she had intended to carry and waited while the girl transferred her things. Lisbeth paused to write something, showed the shop owner, then stuck it in the bag. "Enjoy yourselves," said Mrs. Walters.

Taking Heather's arm, Lisbeth led her out to the street, where gas lamps glowed eerily in the gathering dark. A covered horsedrawn carriage was waiting. The ribbons woven through the horse's braided mane matched the coachman's red jacket. He tipped his top hat and scrambled down to help Heather and Lisbeth climb in.

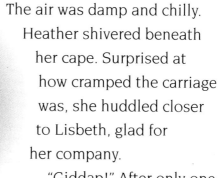

The air was damp and chilly.
Heather shivered beneath
her cape. Surprised at
how cramped the carriage
was, she huddled closer
to Lisbeth, glad for
her company.

"Giddap!" After only one
shake of the driver's reins, the
horse took off down the dusty lane.
Before long the carriage settled into a rocking rhythm,
interrupted only by an occasional lurch or bump.

Heather wondered how far they'd be traveling. She
and Jenna usually sang and played games to pass the
time during family road trips. "Do you like to sing,
Lisbeth?" The girl nodded. "Teach me an English song,
then," Heather said. "And I'll teach you an American one."

Lisbeth taught her "The Man Who Broke the Bank."
Heather had a hard time deciding on a favorite, and
finally settled on a silly camp song, "The Ants Go
Marching." She wished she could see something more
than the silhouettes of trees that sped past the carriage.

Before long, Lisbeth exclaimed, "Heather, look!" She
pointed to a grand fieldstone estate that rose through the
fog and the dark.

Heather was amazed at the size of the house as the carriage rounded the long circular drive. A sharp noise came from up ahead. Their horse suddenly reared, and Heather clutched Lisbeth's arm.

"It is only a motorcar." Lisbeth laughed lightly. "Do not be frightened."

At the front door, the coachman helped the girls alight. Heather shivered in the great, drafty entry hall as a uniformed butler took their capes, then escorted them to a high-ceilinged parlor. There he asked them to wait for Miss Catherine and Lady Spencer-Moulton.

"Oh, wow, look at that!" Heather gaped at the massive crystal chandelier that glittered overhead. Huge potted palms and fancy carved chairs dotted the splendid room. A welcoming fire crackled on the hearth behind a decorative metal screen, taking some of the chill from the air.

Lisbeth clicked the handbag's clasp nervously. "I shouldn't have come, Heather," she whispered.

"Nonsense! We'll have a ball!" Heather grinned at her own joke.

The doors opened

abruptly. Lisbeth dropped a quick curtsy. Before Heather could even wonder whether she should do the same, she was swept into the embrace of a lilac-scented woman and a blond-haired girl who she supposed must be Catherine. "At last we meet. I thought you would never arrive, Heather!" The girl who must be her cousin exclaimed. "Let me have a look. Mother, you see there? Isn't she lovely?"

"She's a vision. Quite so! Heather, your mother's letters do not do you justice. We are so glad you have come. I'm your Aunt Beatrice, of course." The woman squeezed Heather's hands affectionately. "Please, introduce us to your friend."

# C h a p t e r
# Five

# STOLEN!

After the introductions, Catherine narrowed her gaze at Lisbeth and said, "I know you." Then she turned to Heather. "Come along now. My friends have been waiting to meet you."

With Lisbeth tagging after them, Catherine led Heather down a long corridor that opened onto a vast ballroom. It was lined by stately columns that reminded Heather of the ones in the downtown library back home. Shiny platters of sweets and pheasant and lamb covered a long table lit by silver candelabras.

Heather was quickly enveloped by the rustling skirts of several girls her own age. "Oh, Kate, she's a dear!" one girl in a blue gown exclaimed.

"All the way from America? My word," commented another girl.

"And this gown! Like a Southern belle she is."

The girls continued to fuss over her, and Heather's cheeks went hot. Beyond the tables, men in dark tails and stiff-collared shirts escorted the women as gingerly as if they were made of porcelain. The orchestra was tuning up. Even the air smelled fancy and exciting as Heather took it all in.

Suddenly, she remembered Lisbeth. "Did any of you see my friend?" she interrupted the others. "She was wearing a—"

"Oh. Her," one girl replied. "Wasn't she the one carrying the silver candelabra a few minutes ago?"

"I don't know." Heather searched the room. "Will you all please excuse me? I need to go find her."

"Oh, Heather." Catherine sighed. "You've only just arrived. Do you really need to rush off? We've been waiting ever so long to meet you."

"Yes, do stay," one of the girls murmured. "Tell us all about America. Is that where you found this gown?"

Heather was about to explain where the dress had really come from when she noticed Catherine wink and touch a finger to her lips. "It was a gift," Heather hedged. "Aren't I lucky?"

The girls continued to chatter about her ball gown, her hair, and about how very like royalty she looked. Heather, embarrassed, wished they would ask her again about America. Their compliments and instant acceptance made her almost dizzy.

Aunt Beatrice wove toward them through the crowd of formally dressed men and soft-skirted women. She motioned Catherine closer and whispered, "You've forgotten your necklace and bracelet, my dear. Take Heather with you. Show her your room."

Making her apologies to the others, Catherine led Heather from the hall. Near the entry, Heather saw Lisbeth, and the girl turned her face away. Heather's cheeks reddened. How could she have so totally forgotten Lisbeth?

"Come with us," said Heather. "We're going up to Catherine's room."

Lisbeth shook her head, but Heather simply took her hand and ushered her down the hall, ignoring the

scowl on Catherine's face.
Up the grand staircase
they went, their dancing
slippers softly echoing up
the polished stairs.

When they entered Catherine's bedroom,
Heather's eyes went wide at the massive
canopied bed, almost twice as large as her own.
A sturdy wardrobe to the left reminded her vaguely of the
one in Ellie's attic, except for the oval mirror that
adorned its door. Slatted wooden blinds covered the
windows, while lace-edged draperies swooped gracefully
down and were tied to each side. Several framed pictures
dotted the pale-blue, striped wallpaper.

Catherine crossed to her nightstand and took out a
small gold-colored box. Opening the lid, she withdrew an
exquisite pearl bracelet. "Come, Heather," she said, "help
me do it up now, will you?"

"It's beautiful," Heather said.

"Isn't it? It is an heirloom, you know."

Lisbeth faded back toward the wardrobe. She fidgeted
with her bag, plainly nervous. "Miss Catherine, I—"

Catherine looked up in surprise. "I didn't know you
were still here."

"Shall I go?" Lisbeth asked.

"Not without us," Heather said. "We're going back to the ball now ourselves, aren't we, Catherine?"

For a long moment, her cousin admired the bracelet's lustrous sheen and did not reply. Then she looked again in the jewel box and frowned.

"Miss Catherine, please. There is something—"

"Not now, Lisbeth," said Catherine testily, clapping the box shut and putting it away. Closing the door to her bedroom, she escorted the girls downstairs to the ballroom.

Aunt Beatrice was talking to a red-jacketed waiter with a tray of drinks, she turned as Catherine approached. Her delicate eyebrows met in a frown. "Where's your necklace, Catherine?" she asked.

"It wasn't in my jewel case, Mother. I afraid it might be stolen."

"Stolen?" Heather's voice squeaked.

Catherine nodded resolutely.

"Are you sure you didn't just misplace it?" asked Heather. "Maybe you put it somewhere else."

"Catherine is quite careful with her things," Aunt Beatrice said.

"But who would have done such a thing?" Heather persisted. "No one here would—"

"No one?" interrupted Amelia, the tallest of

Catherine's friends, narrowing her eyes at Lisbeth.

"Girls, please," Aunt Beatrice said patiently, then turned to her daughter. "Catherine, when last did you see it?"

"Yesterday. I am sure of it."

Her friends closed ranks beside her, their colorful dresses encircling Heather and Lisbeth. Heather glanced at Lisbeth. Suddenly, her friend looked as nervous as a caged bird. A moment later, Lisbeth was reaching into her bag. "Miss Catherine, please lis—"

"Look at this!" Amelia grabbed a strand of iridescent pearls from Lisbeth's hand. "Come see what our shop girl has in her bag!"

"Omigosh!" said Heather, as the others all gasped.

"Someone *did* see her earlier with a candelabra," one girl reminded them.

Lisbeth burst into tears. "Listen to me, please," she managed at last. "I—I can explain."

"What is there to explain?" asked Amelia, holding the necklace before Lisbeth's tearful eyes.

Chapter

# Six

# A TOUGH
# DECISION

L isbeth looked as if she might bolt. But Aunt Beatrice
touched her arm and told her to wait. "Heather," her
aunt asked gently, "how well do you know this girl?"

Heather glanced at the others, unsure whether to stand
by Lisbeth or not. "I—I just met her, at the dress shop,"
Heather said finally. "She's an orphan, from St.
Philomena's. But the shop owner trusts her. And I liked her
right away. She seemed like such a hard worker, and she's
so nice. I might have misjudged her, but . . ." She ended

with a shrug. They'd found the necklace right there in Lisbeth's purse. If she hadn't taken it, then how could it have gotten there?

Aunt Beatrice thanked Heather for the information, then took Lisbeth aside and let the girl speak. After a few moments, Lisbeth pulled a piece of paper from her bag and showed it to Aunt Beatrice.

Meanwhile, Catherine consoled Heather. "It is not your fault," she said. "You meant well, befriending her. How could you know her true nature?"

"I—I thought I did."

"Things here are different from America," Amelia said. "One does not often find shop girls at charity balls."

"How could Heather know that?" another girl murmured. "She has no blame in this."

A short, red-haired girl spoke next. "Can you believe the nerve of that girl, standing right here in our midst with Kate's necklace." She touched her own necklace, a cameo on a velvet ribbon, as if to reassure herself that it was still there. "Is anything else missing, I wonder?"

As the girls checked their jewelry, Heather glanced again at Aunt

Beatrice. What would become of Lisbeth? Would Aunt Beatrice turn her out into the night? Would she call the police? Heather wondered how she could have been so wrong about somebody.

Music was playing now—a waltz, she thought—and Heather wished she could regain her earlier excitement. No one seemed to have noticed the commotion over Catherine and Lisbeth, and many of the adults were dancing, whirling in circles. Boys clustered in the far corner of the hall. It didn't seem right even to notice them, though, when things looked so bleak for Lisbeth.

"Come, Heather," Catherine was saying. "You haven't met your cousin William." She pointed to a tall, fair-haired boy across the room.

"But I—" Heather faltered. "What about Lisbeth? Shouldn't we at least . . ." The girls stared at her in disbelief, and Heather backed off. She didn't want to turn them against her. They'd made her feel so special from the moment she'd entered the ballroom. "Never mind."

Catherine led her along the refreshment table, where they sipped sweet pink punch and sampled tiny frosted pastries. "Here comes William," whispered Catherine. "He is nicer than he looks."

Heather giggled. Cousin William, who was probably a few years older than she was, could have been

Cinderella's Prince Charming. After the introductions, William asked Heather to dance. Unfortunately, she was too busy trying to count one-two-three, one-two-three in her head and keep her feet out of his way to fully enjoy herself. Besides that, the sharp scent of the carnation in his lapel tickled her nose. How embarrassing it would be to sneeze right in his ear!

When the music stopped, Heather joined the others in clapping politely. She wished she could think of something to say to William, especially since she had only just met him. But her thoughts kept wandering to Lisbeth and the necklace. What could Aunt Beatrice and Lisbeth still be discussing? "Will you excuse me, please?" she asked at last. "I need to go talk to Catherine."

William's dimple deepened into a smile. "Certainly."

He escorted Heather back to Catherine, then excused himself. One of the dancers was motioning for Aunt Beatrice. She patted Lisbeth's arm and left her beneath a marble arch, looking as pale as her dress. With Aunt Beatrice out of earshot, the other girls were moving toward the shop girl now, with Catherine in the lead. Heather went with them, though she had no idea what they—or she—were going to do.

# Chapter
## *Seven*

# TRUE FRIENDS

At least let's hear her explanation," Heather blurted out, to everyone's surprise—including her own.

Catherine sighed. "If you think we must, Heather."

All eyes riveted on Lisbeth. The tiny blond seemed to grow even smaller as she fumbled in her purse. Heather felt suddenly protective and inched closer. With trembling fingers, Lisbeth withdrew a folded piece of paper.

"Miss Catherine, you see, it is what I tried to tell you earlier." Lisbeth handed her the sheet, but Catherine didn't even bother to look at it. "I found the necklace yesterday, in the pocket of the dress you brought in for repair. I had intended to return it directly to you so your mum wouldn't scold you for being careless." She half smiled at Heather. "But when Miss Heather here invited me to the ball, I thought . . ." Her voice trailed off.

Heather strained to read the note but the cramped handwriting would have been hard to decipher, even right side up.

"I—I didn't want to embarrass you, Miss," Lisbeth said, averting her gaze.

"How do you explain the candelabra, then?" one of the girls demanded. "What were you doing with that?"

Lisbeth's eyes again welled with tears. She rubbed at her nose. Heather handed her a handkerchief. "I only borrowed it, and with permission, of course," Lisbeth said. "I wanted to have a closer look at the signature on that painting." She indicated an ornately framed portrait near the entry. "I thought it said Atkins, like my surname."

"That is a strange thing to do," Amelia said.

"Not so strange, Miss, when one is an orphan." Lisbeth smiled thinly. "In truth, I felt so unwelcome and hadn't a clue what to do with myself. I thought, what harm could there be in looking about, in getting away for a few minutes?" She angled her chin, meeting her

accusers with a steady gaze, then turned again to
Catherine. "I should have told you about the necklace
earlier, Miss, but for your own sad treatment of me. I
hadn't the opportunity."

"Read the note," Heather urged her cousin.

A hush fell over the girls, and Catherine finally read it
aloud. "Found this day in the pocket of one blue velvet
gown, brought in for repair by Miss Catherine Spencer-
Moulton, one pearl necklace with gold clasp. Released by
Mrs. Cornelia Walters for return in the person of Miss

Lisbeth Atkins." The note was signed by the shop owner, and by Lisbeth, too. Catherine's cheeks flushed. "Please accept my apology, Lisbeth."

"Yes, and ours," murmured the other girls after a moment's pause.

It had been so easy to be swayed by what the others thought. Heather silently scolded herself for having doubted Lisbeth—and her own instincts.

"I should like to go now," Lisbeth said.

"No, please," Catherine replied, "I would like you to stay. And I know Heather would, too."

"You can say *that* again." Heather laughed at the confused looks on the girls' faces. "That's American for 'most definitely.'"

Heather didn't catch up with Lisbeth, who was much in demand, until after Heather had danced several times with William and his friends. She suspected that the flush of excitement in the shop girl's cheeks mirrored her own.

"It is marvelous, isn't it?" Lisbeth giggled. "How shall I ever thank you, Heather?"

"*Thank* me? I was worried about you *forgiving* me," said Heather. "I didn't mean to ignore you. Really I didn't. I just got so swept up in—," her gesture included the ballroom, the departing dancers, the table now almost

bare of treats, and particularly Catherine and her friends,
"—all this."

"I can't fault you for that."

"I wish you *would*. I really wasn't a very good friend."

"Please, Heather, you needn't go on so."

"Okay." Heather took Lisbeth's hands. "Look, there's
something I have to do now. So if you can't find me later,
don't worry. Just ask the coachman to take you home."

"But—"

Heather cut her off with a quick hug. She let the
kaleidoscope of music and remaining couples imprint
itself in her mind. She would save it for
later, for when she shared it with Megan,
Keisha, and Alison. Now, she gave
Lisbeth a parting smile, then hurried off
to Catherine's room to write a thank-you
to the Spencer-Moultons.

Heather propped the note on
Catherine's desk and took one last look
around. Then, she approached the oval
mirror on the door of the wardrobe,
gazed into her reflection, and closed
her eyes. When she opened them
again, Ellie's familiar gilt-edged
mirror greeted her. The warm glow

of the attic caressed her bare arms.

How alone Heather felt after having been surrounded by Catherine and her friends and all those dancing couples! She could hardly wait to find Ellie and talk about the ball. It didn't take long to change her clothes and come clattering out of the attic, clutching the key in her hand.

The doors to the living room were open. Ellie was sipping a glass of iced tea and reading the afternoon newspaper. Heather put the key away and went in.

"Ah!" Ellie said, setting the paper aside. "I see you're back."

"I was in olden-day England," Heather announced, "at a charity ball."

Ellie patted the space beside her on the sofa and Heather sat down. When Ellie raised a questioning eyebrow, Heather went on. "I invited a shop girl named Lisbeth to go with me."

"That was generous of you," said Ellie, tucking a hairpin back into her silvery French twist. "I suppose I learned generosity from my father. He contributed to a lot of charities in this town, and I've tried to continue where he left off."

Heather thought of the artwork her mother had been asked to donate to the Children's Hospital auction. "Don't you worry about needing that money yourself?"

Ellie waved away her concern. "That doesn't bother me. Besides, I'm repaid many times over, in many ways."

"I sure wish I'd been more generous," Heather said. "I wasn't a very good friend to Lisbeth, not once we got to the ball." Now that she thought of it, she probably hadn't been a very good friend to Megan, Alison, and Keisha. She'd been so quick to accuse them of being jealous, when probably they were only telling her a hard truth. Her parting words rang hollowly.

Ellie eased a strand of Heather's long hair off her face. "I have utmost faith in you, dear." The chimes echoed in the entry hall. "Oh, my! Time for another student."

Heather stood up and headed for the door. "Thanks, Ellie," she called over her shoulder. "See you soon, I hope."

Long shadows from Ellie's picket fence and budding trees were gathering outside. Heather bit her lip as she passed Alison's house. Before she went to apologize to her friends, there was something she had to do.

Heather played with the telephone cord, her pulse racing. What was she going to say? Was it too late to change her mind and simply hang up?

Tiffany's voice, high and light, drifted through the receiver. "Heather? Is that you?"

"Yes." Heather could barely get the word out. "I'm

calling about your party."

"You can come, can't you?"

"I—I'm sorry," Heather said. "I really want to go. It's just that . . . ." As she struggled for an excuse, Catherine's friends popped into her mind. They'd acted as if Heather were one of them. And yet, she'd heard their nasty whispers about Lisbeth's dress. *Heather's* dress, actually. Would they have been so accepting if *she* had been wearing it? She knew Megan, Keisha, and Alison would have. But she couldn't say the same thing for Tiffany—at least not with any certainty.

"Heather?"

Heather cleared her throat. "Thanks for inviting me, but my friends and I already have plans for that night," she said. All at once another thought struck Heather. What if those plans no longer included *her*?

# Chapter
## *Eight*

# PARTY
# GIRLS

Heather charged past the rocker in the living room. "Where are you off to *now* in such a hurry?" her mother asked.

"To Alison's again," replied Heather. "I've decided not to go to Tiffany's party."

Mrs. Hardin set aside the novel she had been reading. "That must have been a hard decision," she said. "I know how much you wanted to go."

Heather shrugged. "I'd rather be with my *real* friends."

She doubted she could explain to Mom how she'd come to have a change of heart—not without telling her about the charity ball. "I wish I could take Keish, Ali, and Megan somewhere special, though," she said wistfully. "Someplace fancy, where we'd all get to dress up . . ." As her voice trailed off, she looked intently at her mother, and suddenly an idea flashed through her brain.

Her mother frowned. "Heather, why are you—"

"Donate that painting, okay? Oh, please! And let us all come with you to the auction."

Her mother grinned. "That's a great idea, honey. Let's do it. I'll call and get tickets tomorrow."

"Thanks, Mom." Heather gave her a quick hug, sending the chair rocking. "You're the greatest." Then she raced to Alison's, where she found her friends at the kitchen table, serving up Mrs. McCann's fruit tart.

"Want some?" Alison offered.

"Thanks."

Megan pulled out a chair, and Heather sat down. It

seemed like forever before anyone spoke again. Then they all spoke at once: "I'm sorry." They grinned at one another and giggled.

"Me first," Heather said. "You were right, all of you. It was just pretty hard to see it, you know? I guess it took a trip to the attic to open my eyes."

"I *told* you that's where she was," Keisha said to the others, then turned back to Heather. "So? Tell us. What was it like? Where did you go?"

"I'll tell you everything, I promise. But first, I've got to ask you, can I still come to the party?"

"Of course!" said Megan. "Don't be silly."

Heather relaxed when the others nodded eagerly. "Now for my next question. How would you guys feel about going to a fancy charity auction?"

"For real?" Keisha said. "Is your mom donating something?"

"Yep. And she said we all could come. What do you think?"

"Would we have to dress up?" Alison asked, looking a little glum.

Megan patted her on the back. "Cheer up, Ali. We had fun in the attic, didn't we?"

"Yes, but . . ." Alison sighed. "I don't know about you guys, but I don't have a thing to wear!"

"Who cares what you wear? Clothes don't make the girl," said Heather. "It's more important who you are."

"Whoa!" Keisha laughed. "Where'd that come from?"

Heather grinned. "My adventure, I guess. Megan? Got your notebook? Just wait until you guys hear this!"

The night of the party Heather and her parents picked up Keisha, Alison, and Megan after supper and took them downtown to the Circle Building. Mom's painting, *Ice'scape*, was displayed prominently on an easel in the main hall. Red, purple, and yellow balloons bobbed along the ceiling, and curly-ribbon streamers hung down like dizzy torrents of rain.

"Wow!" exclaimed Keisha. "Look at all this cool auction stuff!"

All sorts of donated items covered the long tables. Heather had never seen such a collection of rare phonograph records, quilts, antiques, jewelry, and overflowing picnic baskets in one place. Something at the end of one table looked strangely familiar. She tugged on Megan's sleeve and

pointed at a tall metal urn with a spigot.
"Why do I think I've seen that before?"
she whispered.

"The samovar, you mean?
Doesn't Ellie have one of those
in the dining room?"

"I—I don't know," Heather said.
"She has so many neat things in her
house . . ."

"Girls," her mother interrupted,
"let's find a table. The auction's
about to start."

Heather's dad pulled out chairs for each of them right
up front near the auctioneer. A few minutes later, a
smooth-voiced man took the microphone. "Before we
begin our auction this evening, I'd like to make a few
important introductions," he said. "The proceeds of
tonight's event will go, of course, to benefit the new burn
unit of Children's Hospital. But the wing itself would not
have been possible without a generous gift from—," he
paused and glanced about the room as if he were looking
for someone, "—the Goodwin family."

*Goodwin* family? Heather and Keisha frowned at each
other. Just then, a whisper of chiffon brushed Heather's
shoulder. She glanced up in surprise. "Ellie!"

"Mind if I join you?" The older woman seated herself beside Heather.

"Ah, there she is," said the announcer, and a spotlight found their table. "Eleanor Goodwin, ladies and gentlemen. And seated with her is our celebrity artist contributor, Sarah Hardin. Ladies, will you please stand?"

As they did, cameras started flashing everywhere, making little black spots before Heather's eyes. One of the photographers rushed forward and motioned for the girls to stand also. "Closer, that's right," she said, though Heather already felt as if she were the filling in a Mom-and-Ellie sandwich. Alison, Megan, and Keisha crowded in, too. "Now smile!"

Heather held her pose. After the flash, the photographer pulled out a little pad and asked for the girls' names.

"Why do you want to know?" Keisha asked.

"I'm with the *Morning Star*." The photographer showed them her press pass. "This might even make tomorrow's front page, if I hurry."

Heather thought of Tiffany and giggled. From the grins on their faces, she knew Keisha, Megan, and Alison were thinking the same thing. "Hurry, then," said Heather with a wink at the others. "But please, make sure you spell our names right."

Diary

Dear Diary,

I guess I have a lot to learn about wanting friends and being one. Things weren't any easier in England back in the early 1900s —I had no idea how hard it was for a shop girl to make friends with anyone she chose!

Things were sure different for kids then. My cousins were raised by special servants called nannies. Catherine and William said they hardly ever saw their parents until they were old enough to have good manners at the dinner table! Before that, they pretty much stayed upstairs in the nursery, learning how to be "proper." Nanny even read them bedtime stories and tucked them in.

I have to confess that I poked around Catherine's room a bit before I left. I loved looking at all her dolls. Some were made of china and others were made of rags. She even had

paper cutouts, and lots of doll clothes. Best of all

was this darling little music box. Guess what it

played when I lifted the lid —the same song

Lisbeth taught me in the carriage!

I hope the ball raised a lot of money for the

orphanage. I never thought much about being

generous until Ellie mentioned it. Mom sure felt

good about how high the bidding went on her

painting, though. And Ellie was amazed at what her

samovar earned for the Children's Hospital, too.

Thank goodness Keisha, Alison, and Megan

forgave me. The charity auction wouldn't have been

nearly as fun without them. We felt so special,

being in the spotlight with Mom and Ellie, too. I can

hardly wait to see our picture in the newspaper!

Luv,

Heather